Andrea's Wish

W9-CPF-284

 1 **P**ut together the LEGO® Miniset to build a cozy home for Jazz the bunny.

 2 **R**ead the story to discover Andrea's secret wish.

 3 **C**omplete the puzzles, games, and activities with the LEGO Friends!

Welcome to our world.

Jazz

My Friends

Hidden Secrets

Sometimes you can tell a lot about a person by what they keep in their room or locker. So after school today, I took snapshots of my friends' lockers when they weren't looking to see what I could figure out about them. ☺ Check out the photos and see if you agree with me!

Posted by: Andrea | Wednesday, 3:36 PM

2 comments

Olivia is so handy.

This is Emma's lucky charm!

I like to blog. But you already know that.

Seashore Games

Olivia invented a fun seashore game to play with her friends while they relax at the beach. Invite one of your friends to play with you!

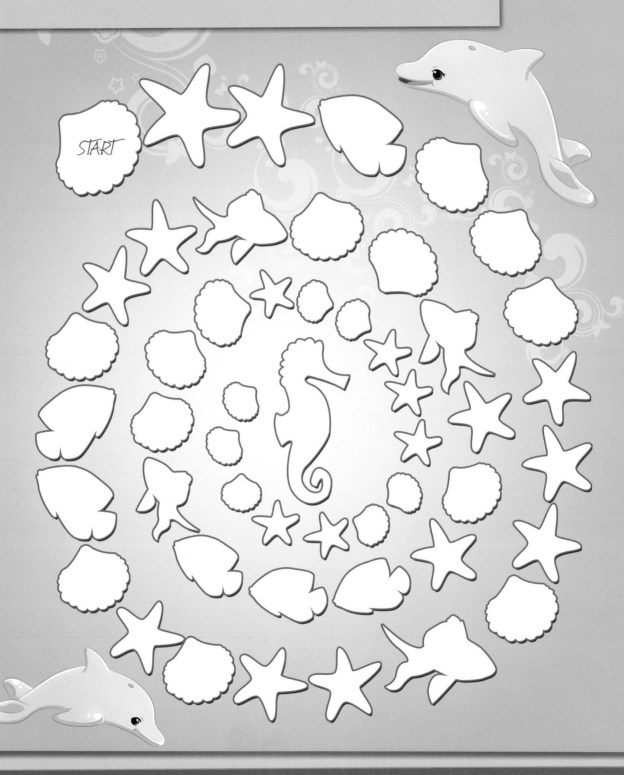

START

Game Rules:

1. Start with two players. Each player chooses one of the boards below.

2. Take turns throwing a die. Color as many spaces on your board as the die shows.

3. **The first person who colors all the spaces on her board is the winner!**
   Remember! When there are less than six spaces left on your board to color, you need to throw the number on the die that matches your number of remaining empty spaces exactly.

Good luck!

START

Andrea's Wish

"That was so much fun!" Andrea exclaimed as she raced inside the house. It was late Saturday afternoon. She had just spent the day with her friends at the beach. They had gone swimming and even spotted some dolphins playing in the water.

"Too bad I can't keep a pet dolphin." Andrea sighed as she emptied the sand from her shoes. "It would be so cute."

That night, as she slept, Andrea dreamed of dolphins. For a long time, she had wanted a pet of her own. Her family had owned a hedgehog once, but he wasn't really Andrea's. Her friends—Mia, Emma, Stephanie, and Olivia—each had special pets that cheered them up when they were feeling down. Andrea knew owning a pet was a big responsibility, but was sure she could handle it!

After the weekend, the friends met at school.

"Girls!" Olivia cried as she ran into the classroom. "A new foal was born at the stables. Aunt Sophie said I can take care of him!"

"What color is he?" Emma asked.

"White," Olivia answered.

"Ooh!" Emma clapped her hands. "Just like my horse, Sunshine! Maybe they can play together."

"Let me know if you need any help taking care of him," Mia chimed in.

"You bet." Olivia smiled. "I definitely have my hands full. My cat, Maxie, chased after the new foal all morning. She wanted to keep up."

"Charlie does that, too." Mia laughed, picturing her puppy.

"Then maybe I should bring Daisy over," Stephanie said. "She loves to hop after everything!"

As the girls were chatting, none of them noticed Andrea had grown quiet. She wanted to join in, but she felt like the only one without a pet. Just as she was about to blurt out "I'm going to get a new pet, too!" their teacher interrupted them.

"May I know what you are all discussing?" she asked. "It must be very important since class has begun."

"Sorry, Ms. Johnson," Stephanie said. "We were just talking about our pets."

"Well, right now it's time to talk about English," the teacher replied. "But I was going to assign an extra-credit essay. Perhaps you girls would like to write about your pets for the project?"

"Sure!" the friends all said together.

After school, the girls ran to the stables to see Olivia's new foal.

"I wish I had a pet, too." Andrea sighed. "You all have pets to write about for your essays. I'll probably have to write about an imaginary pet dolphin."

To cheer up Andrea, the five friends headed to the Downtown Bakery. Each girl chose a tasty pastry. After their snack, Andrea waved good-bye. She had a shift at the City Park Café.

As she strolled down the sidewalk, a squirrel followed her, leaping from tree to tree.

Maybe I'll adopt a squirrel, Andrea thought sadly. She watched it scurry under a bush . . . and suddenly, Andrea spotted a white, fluffy ball of fur. It was a bunny!

"Wow!" Andrea exclaimed.

The bunny looked at Andrea and twitched its nose.

"You must belong to someone," Andrea realized. "Otherwise, you would hop away." She was just about to reach out toward it when Marie called.

"Andrea! Your shift's about to start!"

"I'll be right there!" Andrea replied. She turned to the bunny. "You stay here," she said. "I'll come back for you after I'm done working."

All evening, Andrea tried to concentrate on her customers. But she was too excited about the rabbit she had found to focus. The moment her shift ended, Andrea raced out the door. But by the time she reached the bush where the bunny had been hiding, the little white rabbit was gone.

Story continues on page 14

9

A Sweet Business

In honor of the grand opening of the new Downtown Bakery, we managed to grab a quick interview with the very busy owner and head pastry chef, Danielle Butternut.

HCN: It's only been a few days since you opened, and yet you have everyone talking about your incredible cakes.

DB: Thank you. We love baking and decorating cakes for all sorts of special occasions. My favorite one so far was an octopus-shaped cake for a party held on a yacht. Some of the party guests thought it was a *real* octopus!

HCN: But that's not the only thing your customers are raving about. You also have delicious cookies in fun shapes, like sea horses, starfish, and jellyfish.

DB: The kids really love those. I've always adored baking tasty treats, but what I really enjoy is making them into fun shapes and designs people wouldn't normally expect. We can make a cake or cookie resembling anything you want!

HCN: Really? Could you make, say, a life-size convertible car cake?

DB: *[laughing]* We haven't had that request yet, but we could try. It wouldn't drive like a real car, but it sure would be sweeter than one!

PLAYFUL PETS

The contest is still on for the funniest pet photo **in town. Keep sending us your silly snapshots, and readers can start voting for their favorite pet pictures now.**

Cast your vote by ranking the playful pictures below one through six, with one being the highest.

| 1 | 2 | 3 | 4 | 5 | 6 |

What Do Your Doodles Say?

Everybody loves to doodle, but did you know those tiny drawings can have secret meanings? Find out what your doodles say about you! Take a blank piece of paper and draw some designs without thinking about it too much. Then compare your doodles to the meanings below.

Flowers

Just like **Stephanie**, you're outgoing and cheerful. Your friends can always count on you.

Hearts

You're a romantic at heart just like **Emma**. You daydream of magical, faraway places.

Geometric Shapes

You think logically and make practical decisions the same way **Olivia** does.

Animals

You're very much like **Mia**: open-minded and friendly. People love being around you!

Smiley Faces

You have a great sense of humor and lots of enthusiasm. Like **Andrea**, your smile is contagious.

If none of the patterns above match your doodles, here are some more secret doodle meanings!

Zigzag	– You're very inventive and energetic.
Patterns	– It bothers you when things aren't in perfect order.
Stars	– You are courageous and ambitious.

Tasty Treats

A frosted cake always brightens Andrea's mood. She's chosen the sweet treat below that has three colors, is shaped like a muffin, and has a fruit at the top. Mark the cake you think she picked, then circle the pastry you'd like to eat.

Continued from page 9

"Bunny!" Andrea tried to call the rabbit. "Where did you go?" She whistled.

Suddenly, a dog being walked heard Andrea's whistle and pricked up his ears. He came bounding toward her!

"*Ack!*" Andrea cried as he leapt up and licked her face.

"Sorry," the dog's owner said. "He heard your whistle and thought you were calling for him. You sure have a way with pets."

"It's okay." Andrea laughed. "I just wish the rabbit I was whistling for had come instead."

The next day, as she headed to school, Andrea carried a big bunch of carrots in her arms.

"Oh! You brought carrots for Olivia's horse!" Mia exclaimed when she saw Andrea.

"Not exactly. . . ." Andrea replied. She wanted to tell her friends about the rabbit. But not just yet. "These carrots are for someone else, but I'll tell you all about it tomorrow."

After school, Andrea dashed back to the bush. There was no sign of the bunny, so she left the carrots and hurried to the café.

That evening, she checked the bush again. There was still no bunny, but sure enough, the carrots were gone!

"He must have liked my treat!" Andrea clapped her hands.

The next day, Andrea couldn't keep her secret bunny a secret anymore. She told her friends all about him.

"You should have told us yesterday." Mia frowned. "What if he belongs to somebody? Or is injured? We need to find him and bring him to the vet."

All five girls headed to the bushes by the café.

"He was right in here," Andrea whispered.

Carefully, the girls pushed aside the soft, green branches.

A moment later, their eyes grew wide.

Nestled inside was not just one bunny—but five! A mommy and four babies, all snuggling together.

"Your rabbit isn't a *he*," Mia smiled brightly. "It's a *she*. And she's a new mommy! But this rabbit is definitely someone's pet. Look, she even has a collar. We need to bring her to the vet."

When the girls reached the Heartlake City Vet, they found a woman speaking with Aunt Sophie. The lady looked very worried, and she was holding a flyer with a picture of a lost white rabbit.

"I don't think you need to put up that flyer after all," Olivia said. "We've already found her!"

"Thank goodness!" the owner cried when she saw her missing pet. "And it looks like her baby bunnies are here, too. She was almost ready to have them when she got lost. I was so worried. Thank you girls so much for finding her."

"It was Andrea who saved the day," Mia pointed out. "She saw the bunny hiding in the bushes and brought her food."

"How can I ever thank you?" the owner asked Andrea.

"It was nothing," Andrea insisted. "I loved taking care of her."

"Would you like one of the baby bunnies?" the owner asked. "They'll need to stay with their mommy for a few weeks. But after that, I'd be happy for you to keep one as a pet."

"Do you mean it?" Andrea cried excitedly. "That would be incredible!"

"See?" Mia said with a wink. "Everything worked out. Now you don't have to write about imaginary dolphins after all!"

A few weeks later, Andrea was smiling from ear to ear as she carried her new pet bunny home. Her friends were waiting for her with a rabbit house, a brush, and a big bag of carrots.

"What are you going to call him?" Emma asked, petting the rabbit behind the ears.

"It should be a musical name," Stephanie said. "Maybe Pop? Or Rock?"

"Nah," chimed in Olivia. "It should be something snazzier."

"Yeah," said Andrea thoughtfully. "Or . . . *jazzier*. That's his new name—Jazz!" Andrea giggled as she nuzzled her bunny. "What do you think, Jazz? Do you like that name?"

The little bunny wiggled his nose.

"I think that's a yes!" said Olivia. The five friends laughed.

She Shoots, She Scores!

Have you ever wondered what it would be like to be a sports announcer? Now's your chance! Check out the game recap to the right, and use the clues to figure out the path the ball took before scoring a goal.

Let's see this amazing action once again. **Andrea** dribbled the ball up the field. Then she kicked it to **Stephanie**, who expertly bounced the ball on her knees before passing it to **Olivia**. Olivia dashed toward the ball as fast as she could and just managed to reach it. But she slipped on the wet grass and bumped into **Mia**! The ball bounced off of Olivia's shoe toward **Emma**, who quickly dribbled it away before the other team could steal it. Emma raced down the field and rocketed the ball toward the net, scoring a goal! Three cheers for the **Heartlake High team**!

Sporty Fashion

It's a fashion disaster! The friends' soccer uniforms shrank in the wash. They'll need brand-new outfits for Friday's big game. Use the template below to design sporty new uniforms for them.

Let's get down to work!

Fuzzy Friends

The Heartlake City Vet is overrun with rabbits! Andrea's new bunny, Jazz, is hiding somewhere among them. Can you spot him? Look carefully at the photo of Jazz, and then find the rabbit that matches.

Friends :)   Mommy   Daddy

Emma: *Your bunny has the sweetest spot on its nose ever!*

Andrea: *What do you mean?*

Emma: *Can't you see? The brown one.*

Andrea: *Hmmm . . . it's literally sweet. He's dirty with chocolate.* 😊

Rabbit Lover's Corner

A rabbit starter kit

food dispenser

drinking bottle

carrots

cage

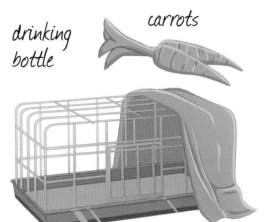

bowl

Check the circles next to the sentences which describe you best. The more sentences that you check, the more likely a bunny is the perfect pet for you!

- I'm patient and understanding.
- I have a good sense of humor.
- I enjoy spending time at home.
- I don't mind playing on the floor.
- I'm responsible.
- I love watching animals.

Talk with your rabbit

Even though rabbits can't talk, you can learn a lot about them from their body language. Check out the below rabbit "dictionary" to see what your bunny is telling you.

If your rabbit:

1. Touches your arm with his nose, he's saying, "I'm curious."

2. Licks your hand, he's saying, "I love you!"

3. Hops all around the room, he's saying, "I'm happy."

4. Turns his back to you and puts his ears down, he's saying, "I'm angry."

5. Closes his eyes when you pet his cheeks, he's saying, "That feels great!"

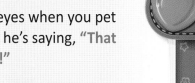

Draw Jazz

Everybody knows that bunnies are super-cute. Why not try to draw one? It's as easy as 1, 2, 3!

Pretty Pet Pictures

A photo of you and your pet is a great way to decorate your room, especially if you display it in a homemade frame. Check out Emma's picture-perfect inspiration!

These may seem like ordinary buttons, but when glued to a frame, they create an amazing effect, don't they?

If you prefer, you can put any favorite picture into your personally designed frame. Just remember, the best picture is one that makes you smile.

You will need:

- a favorite photo
- a frame cut out of cardboard
- glue or double stick tape
- buttons, fabric, string, etc.

Try wrapping colorful yarn around your frame to add pretty pizazz!

Snip pieces of patterned fabric and glue them to your frame for a tailored look.

A handful of seashells, a piece of string, and some glue is all you need for a beach-inspired frame.

Heartlake High News

Casting Call

The Heartlake High Theater Club is calling all students to audition for the next school production of **The Big Game**, a musical comedy about an actress and a soccer star who fall in love. Auditions will be held in the auditorium on Tuesday at 3 PM.

Posted 6 hours ago   25 notes

Tagged: <u>Audition</u>, <u>The Big Game</u>

Go, Team!

The contest for a new soccer team mascot is over. You have chosen Frank the friendly Heartlake High squirrel! Congratulations and good luck to our talented team in the upcoming playoffs. Go, **Heartlake High**!

Posted 3 hours ago   15 notes

Tagged: <u>Frank</u>, <u>New Team Mascot</u>, <u>Heartlake High</u>

Costume Ball

The annual school costume ball is rapidly approaching, and as has been done every year, the school seniors have selected a theme for the event. This year's theme is Carnival! Break out your feathers and maracas, and come prepared for a fantastic party time!

Posted 1 hour ago   32 notes

Tagged: <u>Costume Ball</u>, <u>Heartlake High Ball</u>

Contest

It's time for another teacher contest! Cast your votes for the Most Creative Teacher, Quirkiest Teacher, and Funniest Teacher below.

Music Teacher –
Mrs. Masson

SUBMIT

Physics Teacher –
Mr. Skipper

SUBMIT

Art Teacher –
Mrs. Ferguson

SUBMIT

Design your own mask here:

Olivia's Diary

I always jot down funny stories and cute quirks about my pets in my diary. Read what I wrote about my new foal, Snow. Then tell us all about your perfect pet!

Name: Snow

Animal: Horse

Distinctive marks: Bright white mane

How did I get him: He was a newborn foal at the stables, and Aunt Sophie asked me to watch over him!

Favorite snacks: Carrots and lumps of sugar

Favorite activity: Racing around the meadow together

He is happy when: I make him flower garlands. I know he nibbles on them when I'm not watching.

He's sad when: I'm ill and can't play with him.

The best thing about him is: I can tell him all my secrets, and he'll never say a word to anyone! ☺

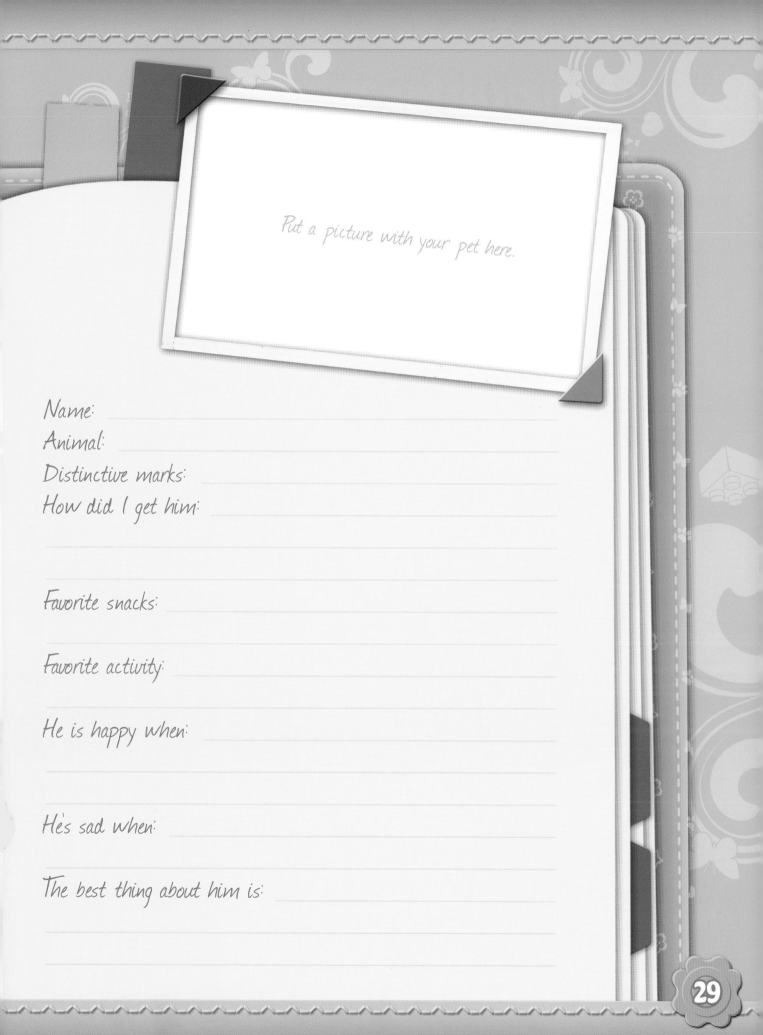

Put a picture with your pet here.

Name: _____

Animal: _____

Distinctive marks: _____

How did I get him: _____
_____

Favorite snacks: _____

Favorite activity: _____

He is happy when: _____
_____

He's sad when: _____

The best thing about him is: _____
_____

Spot the Difference

Andrea's new bunny, Jazz, has been very mischievous. Look at the two pictures of Andrea's room below. Can you spot ten differences between the pictures that hint at what Jazz has been up to?

Friends :)   Mommy   Daddy

Emma: Andrea, you have a gorgeous bedspread!

Stephanie: But wait. Didn't it use to be pink?

Andrea: Yeah . . . I accidentally washed it along with my purple pajamas. Now they're both purple! 😉

* a dresser
* a laptop
* posters
* a violet bedspread
* a heart-shaped pillow

How do you like Andrea's room?
Put a "✓" on the list next to all the objects
which you'd like to have in your own room.

Answers

Tasty Treats — p. 13

Fuzzy Friends — p. 21

She Shoots, She Scores! — p. 18-19

Spot the Difference — p. 30-31

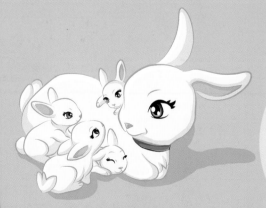